The Pets

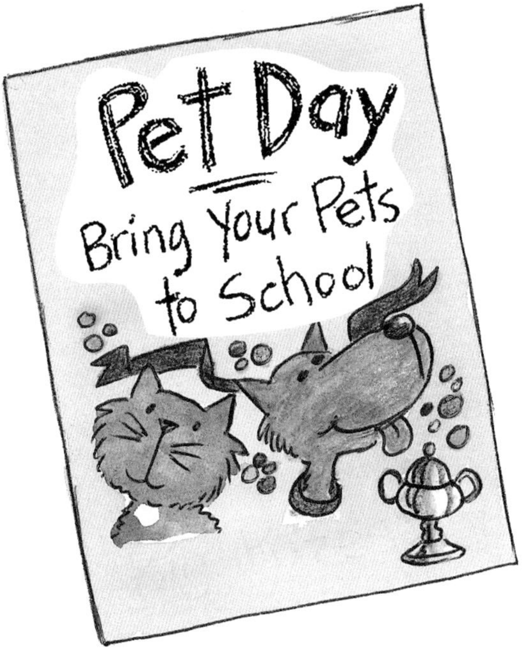

Illustrated by Trevor Pye

Rigby

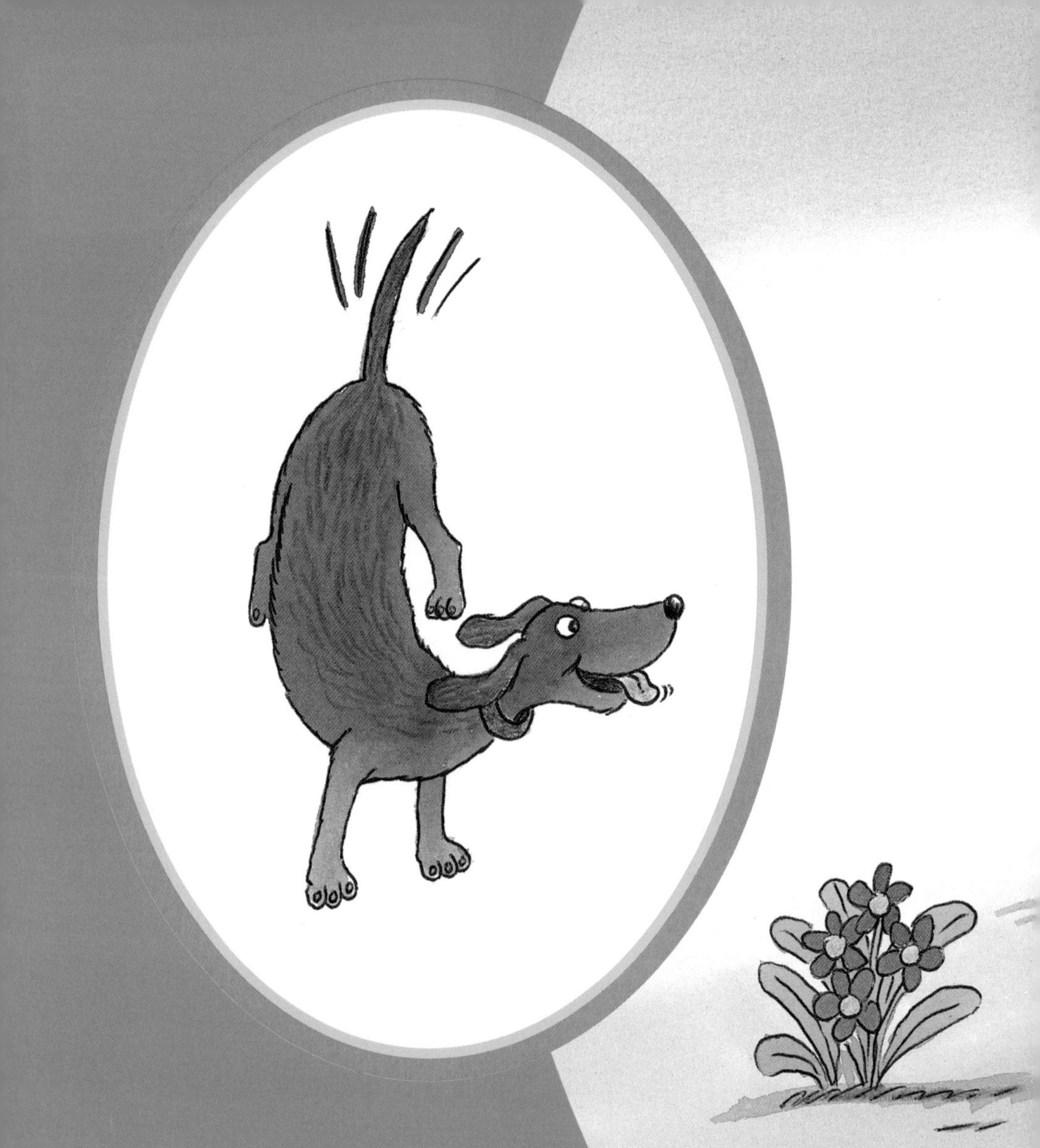

Look at the dog.

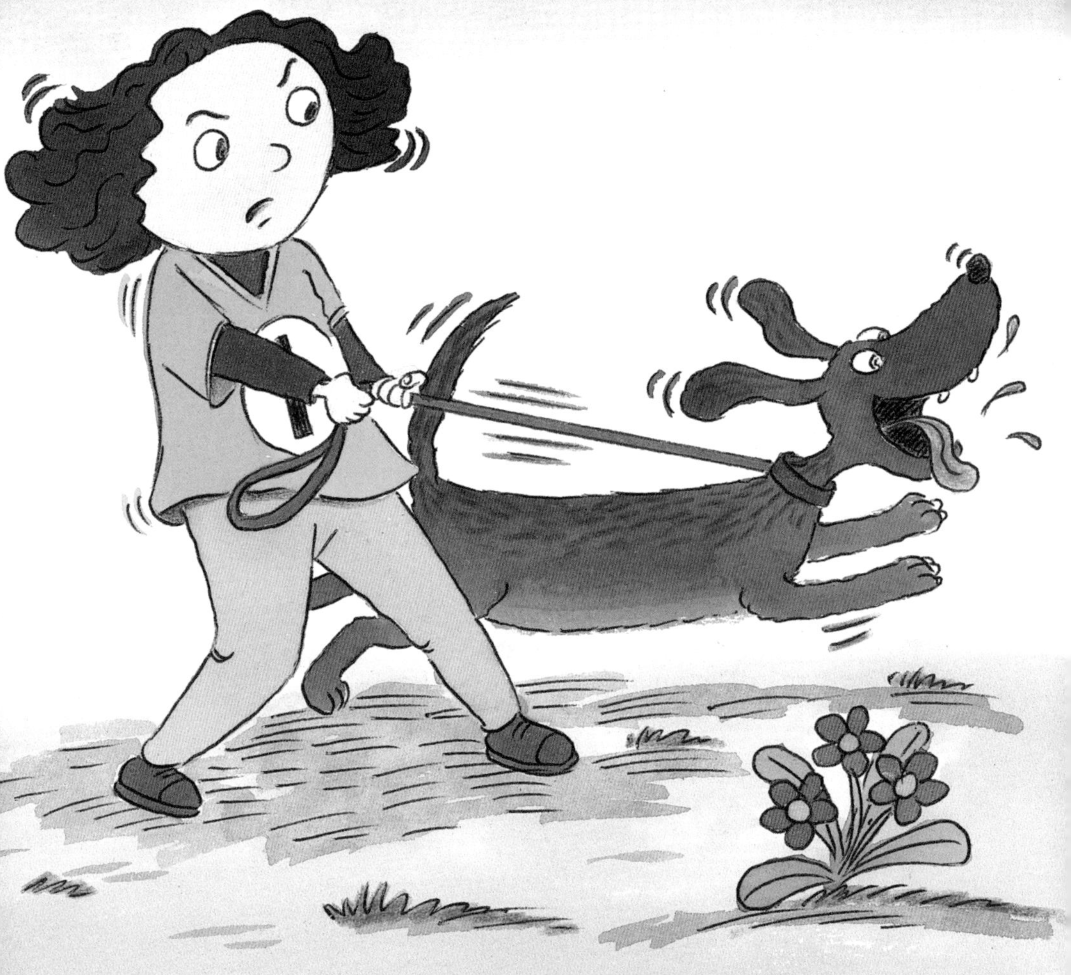

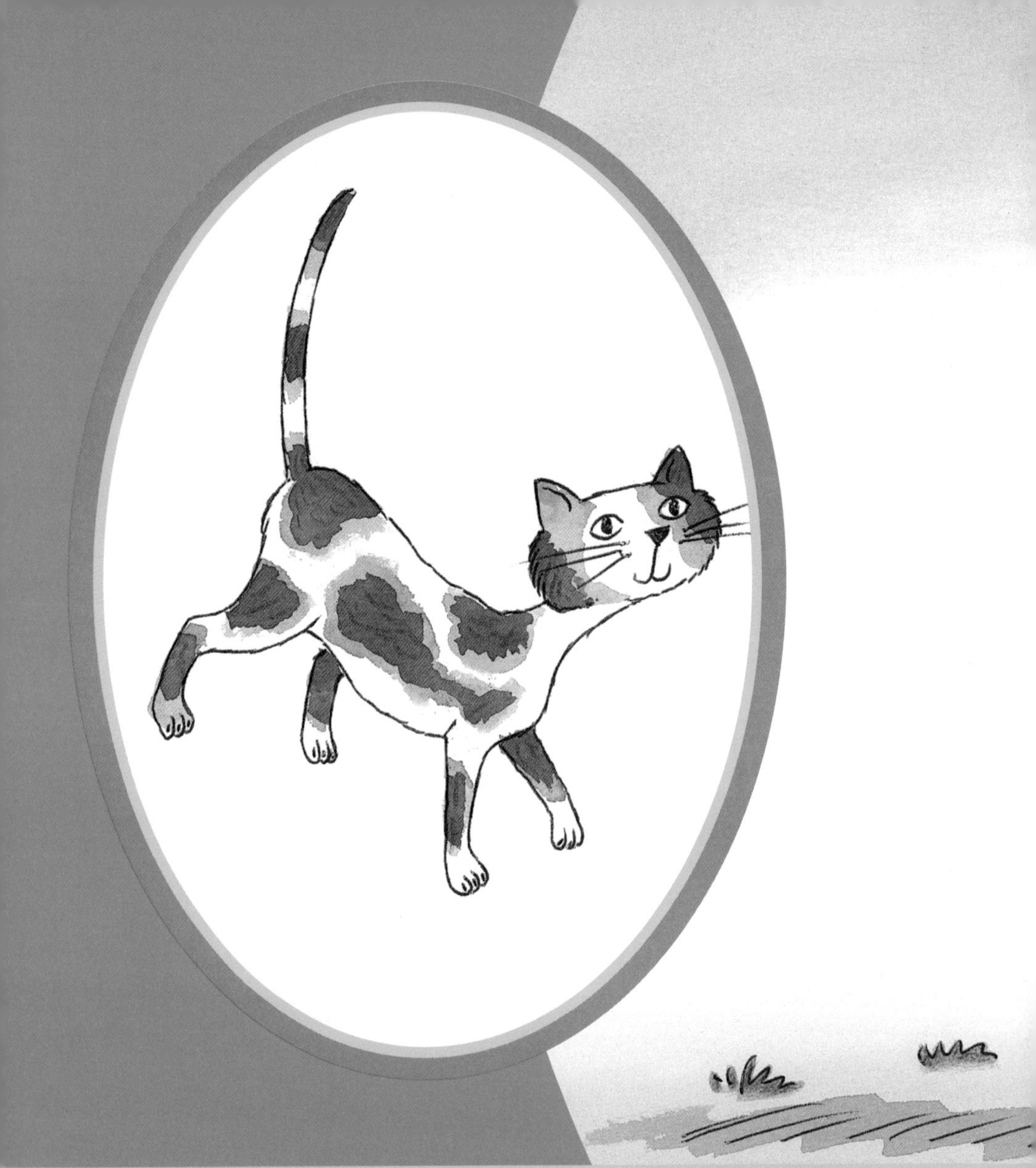

Look at the cat.

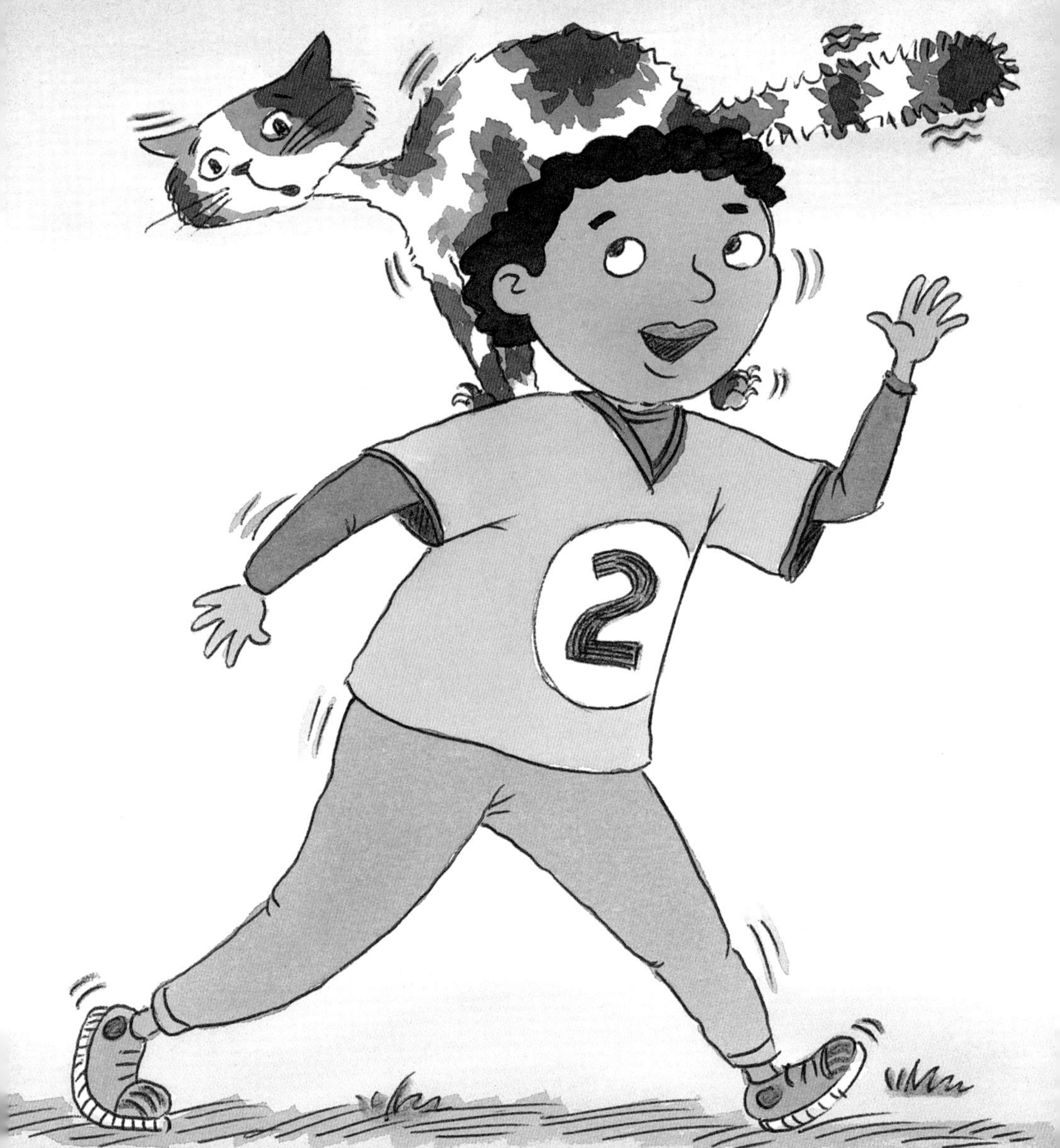
2

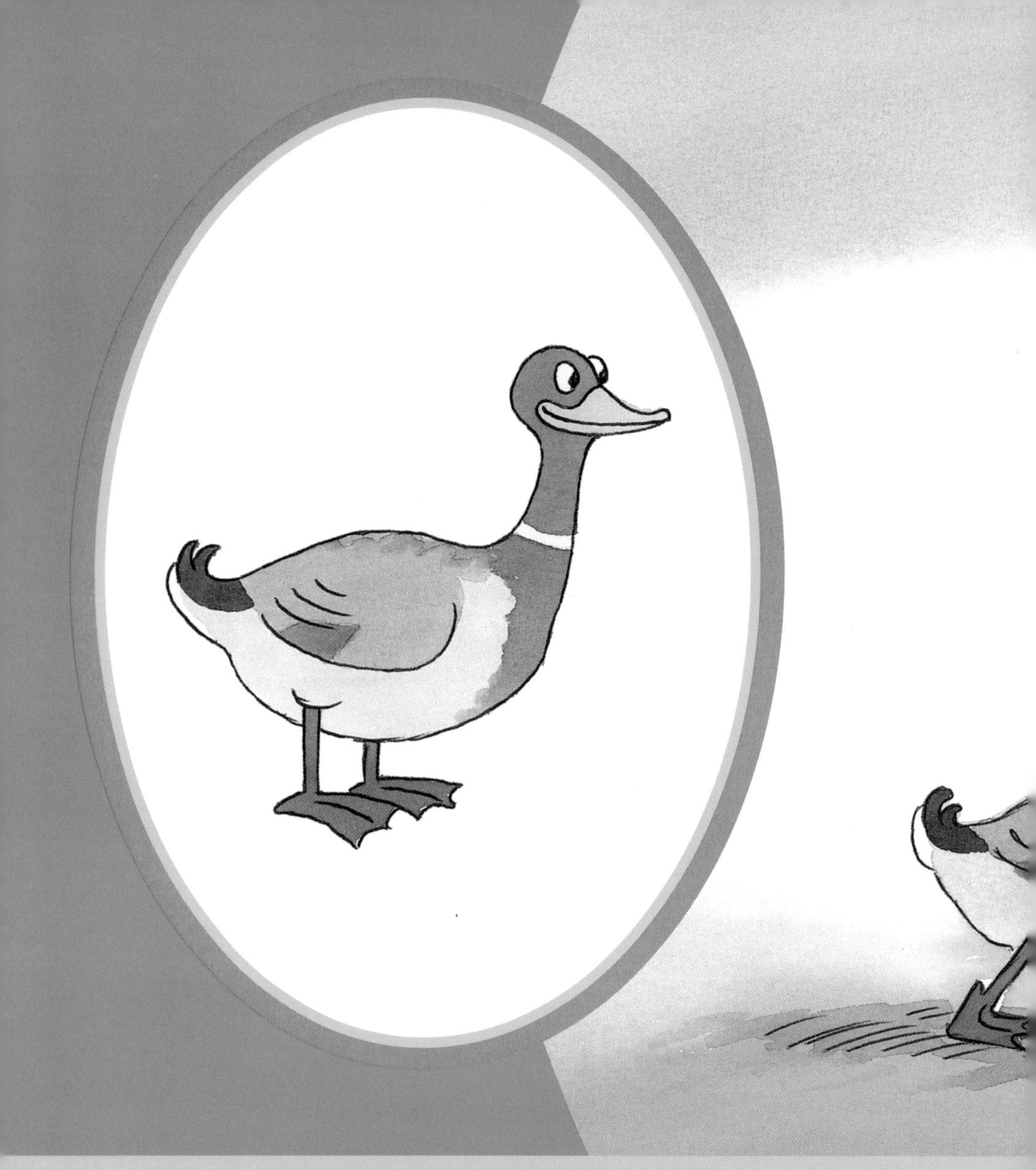

Look at the duck.

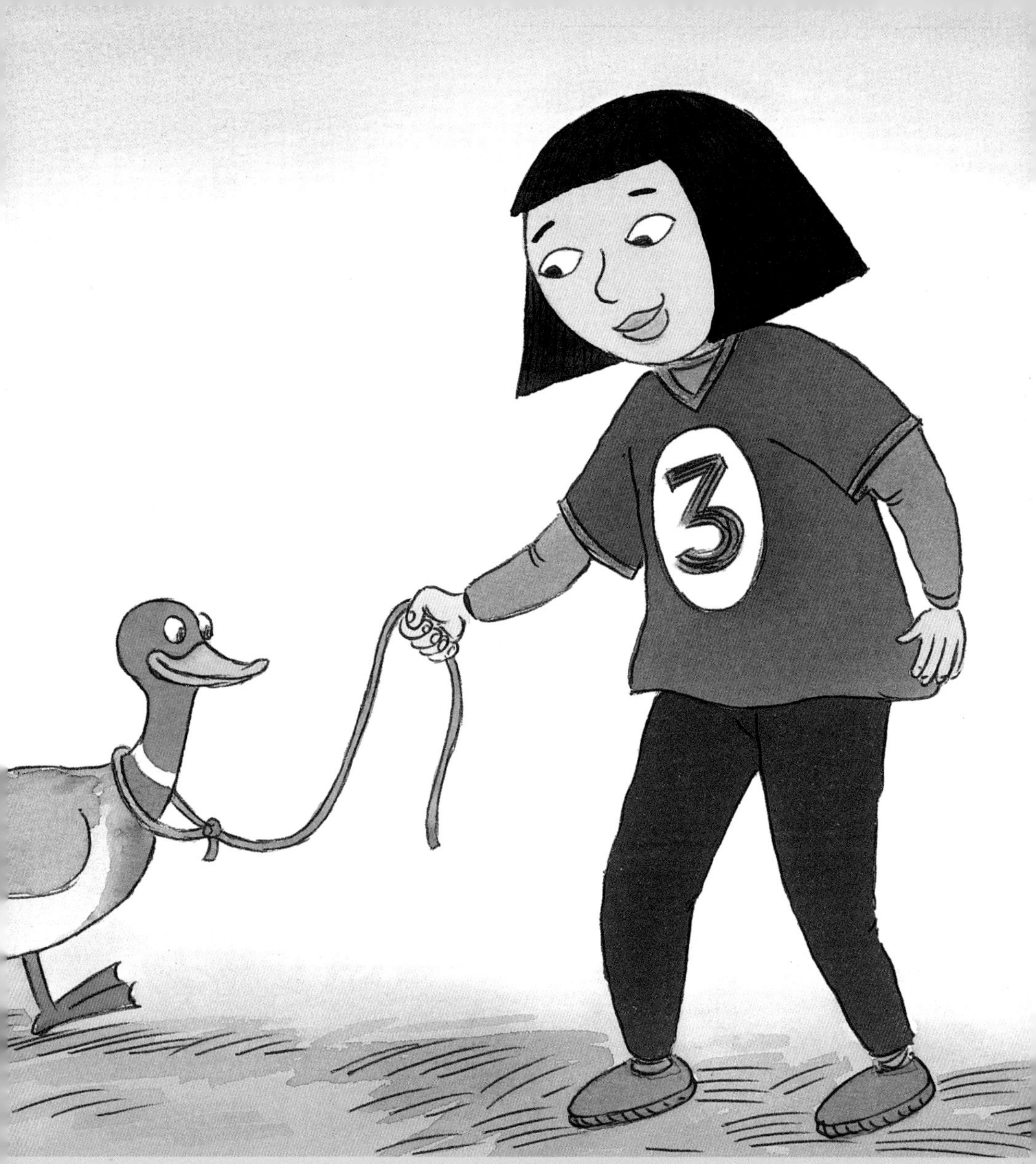
3

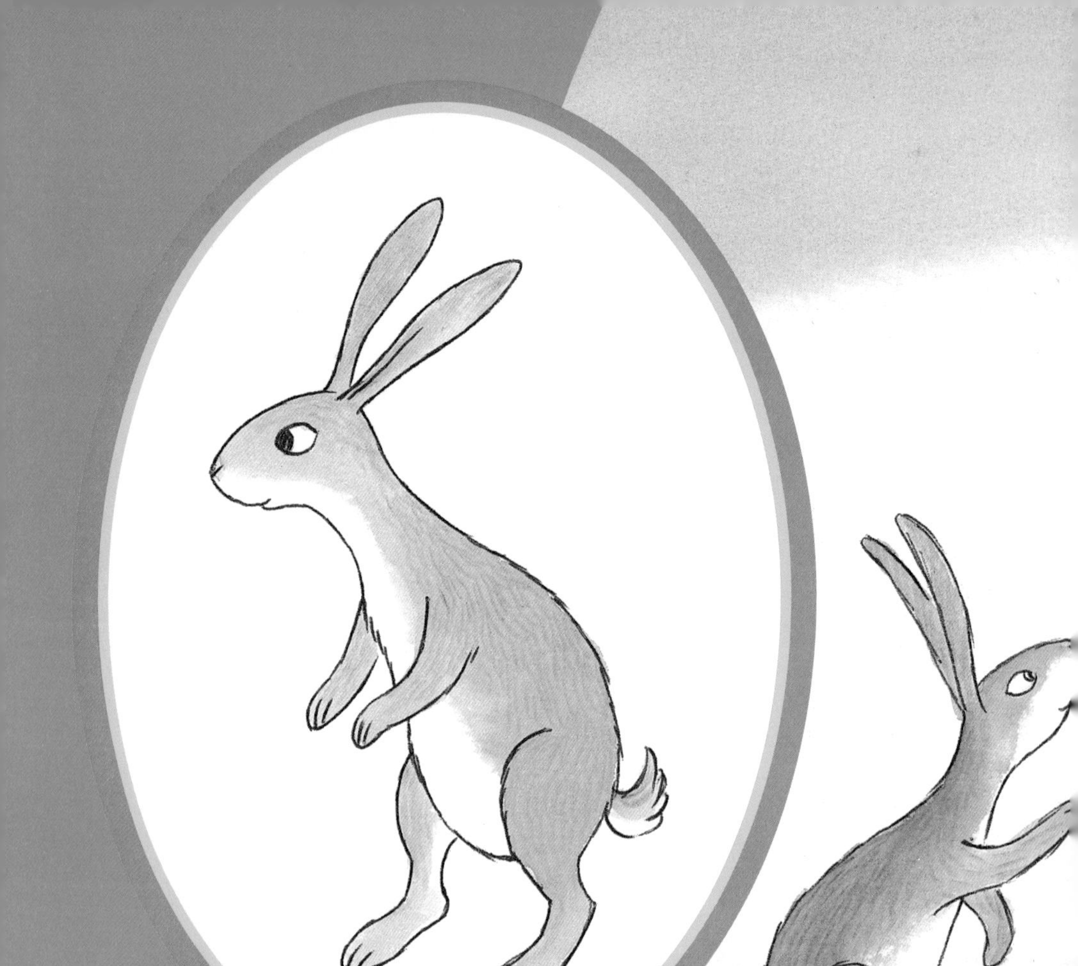

Look at the rabbit.

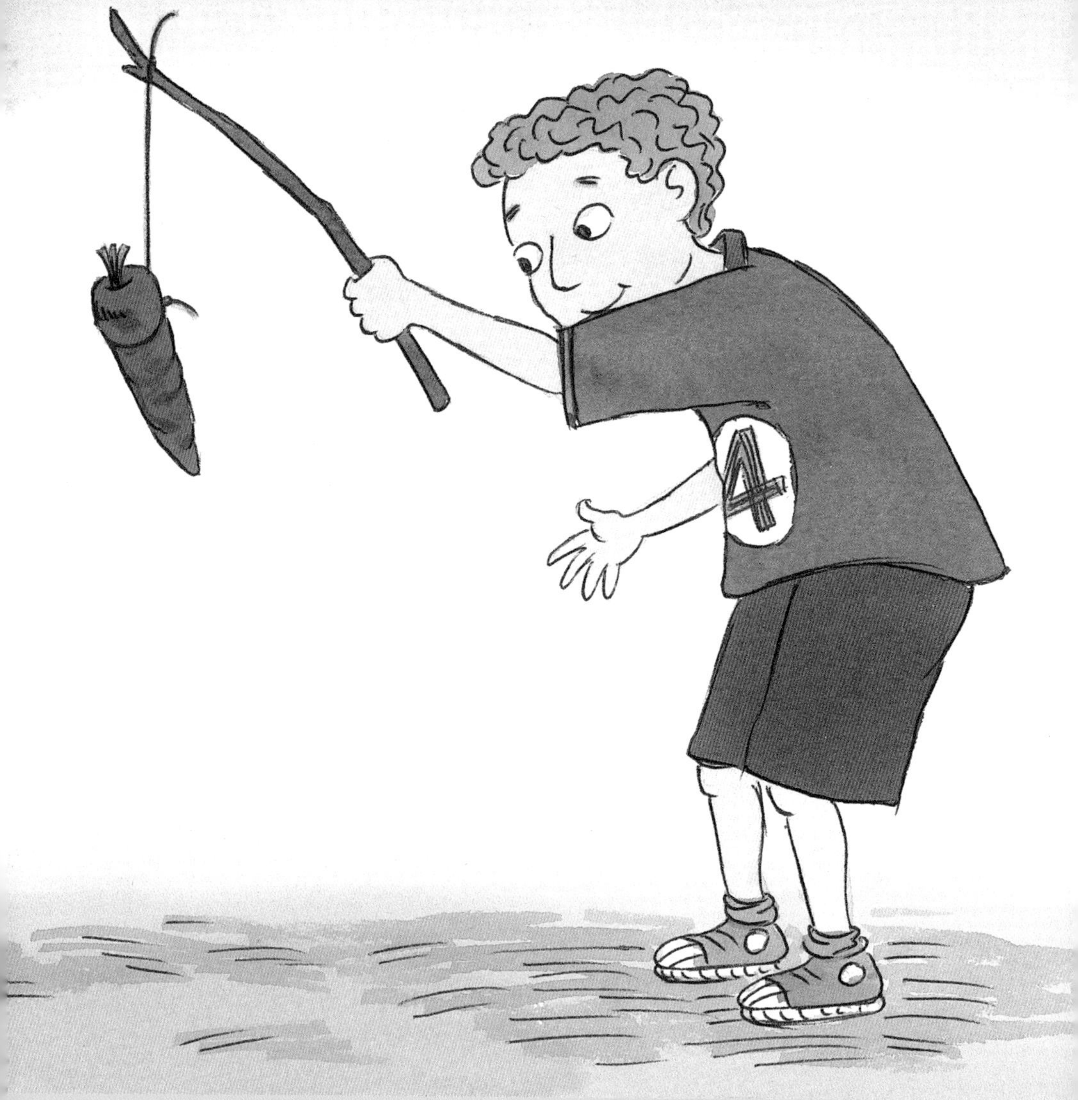
4

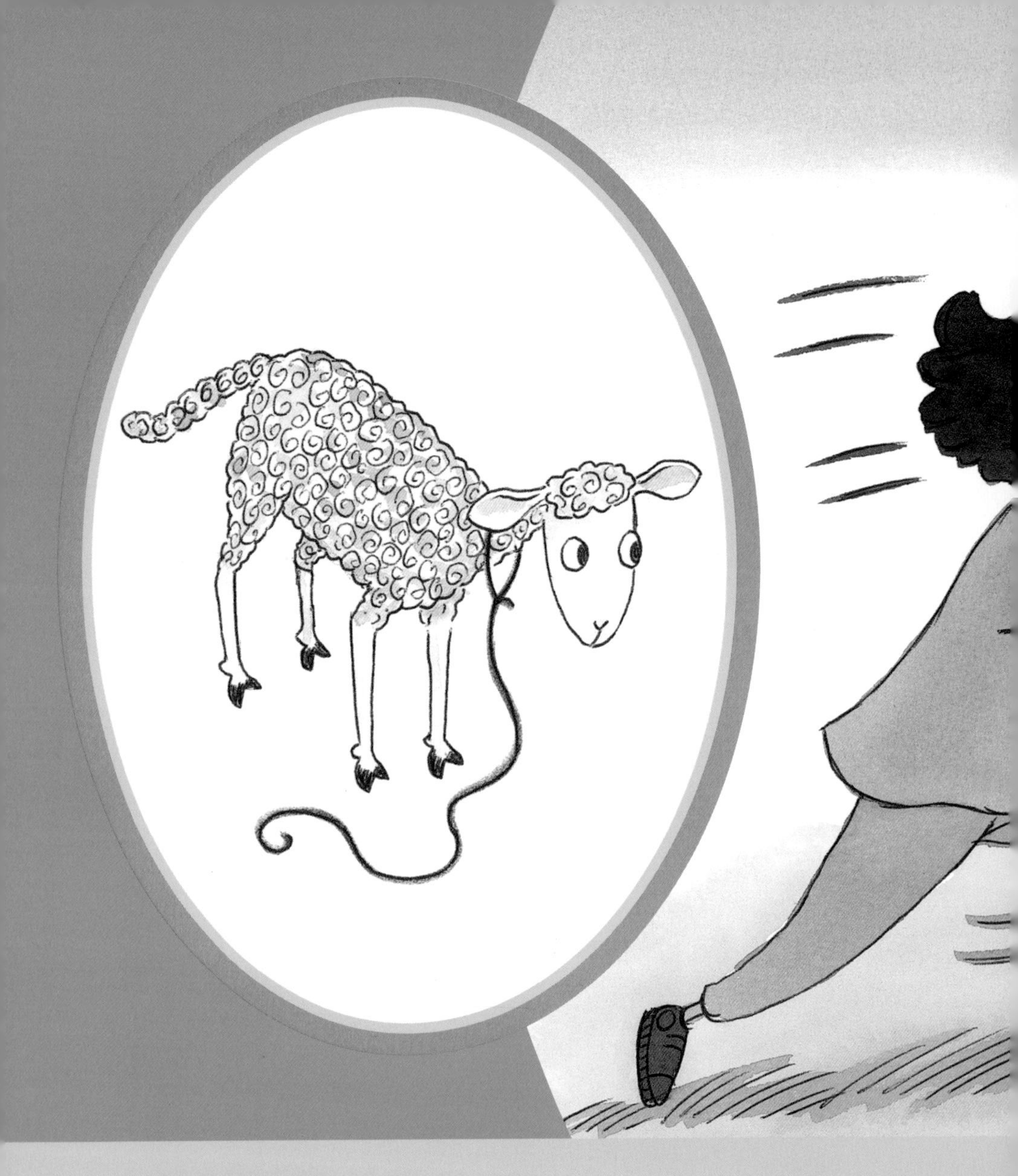

Look at the lamb.

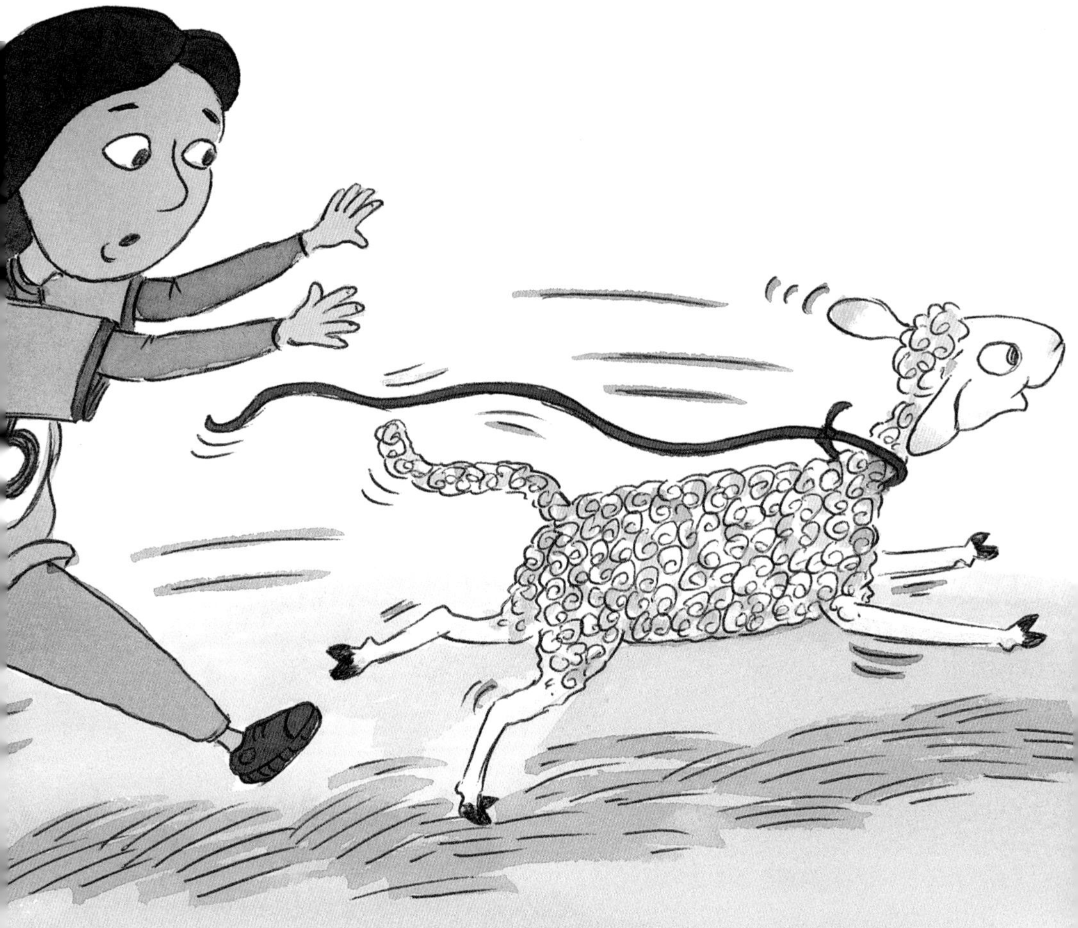

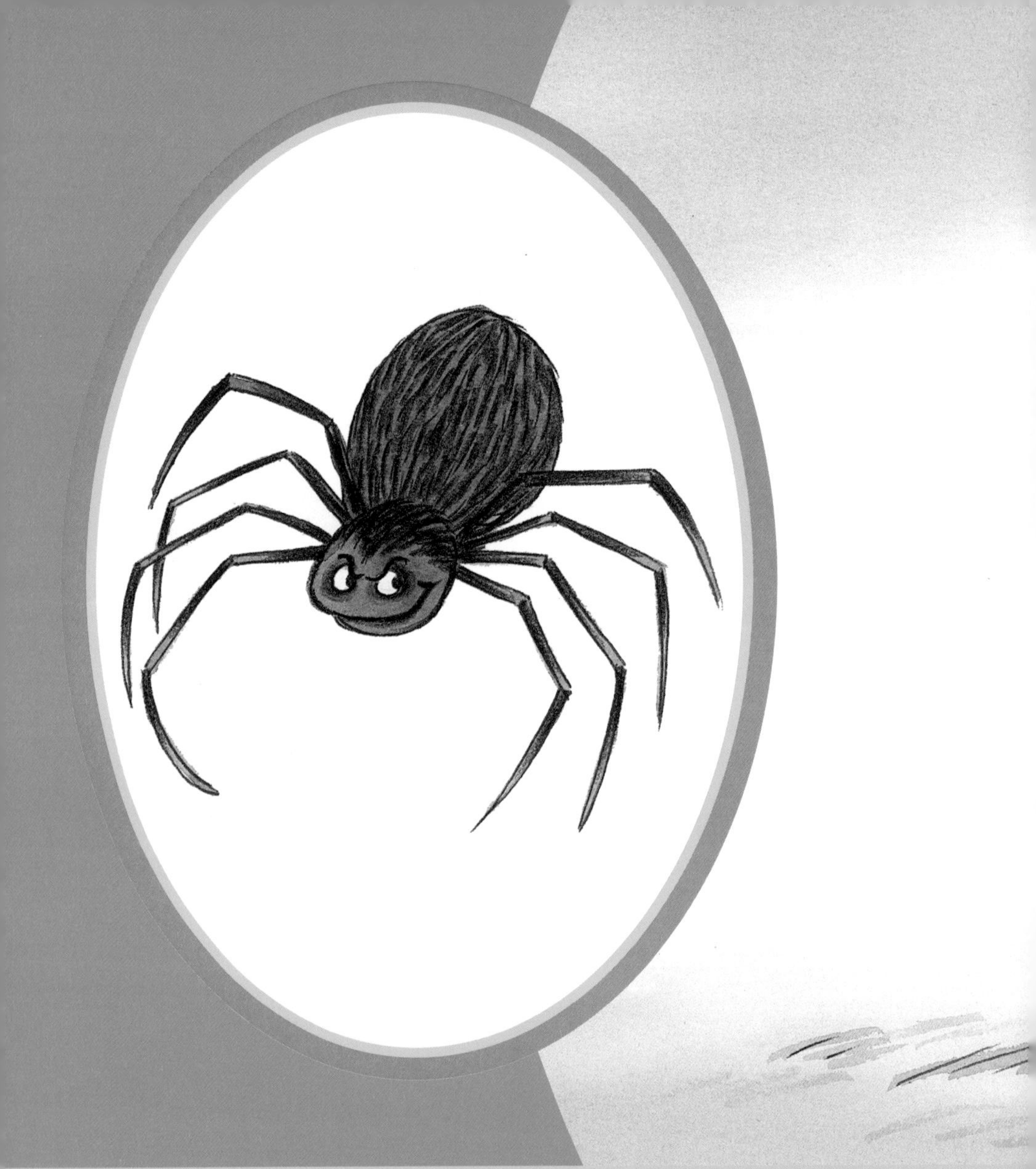

Look at the spider.

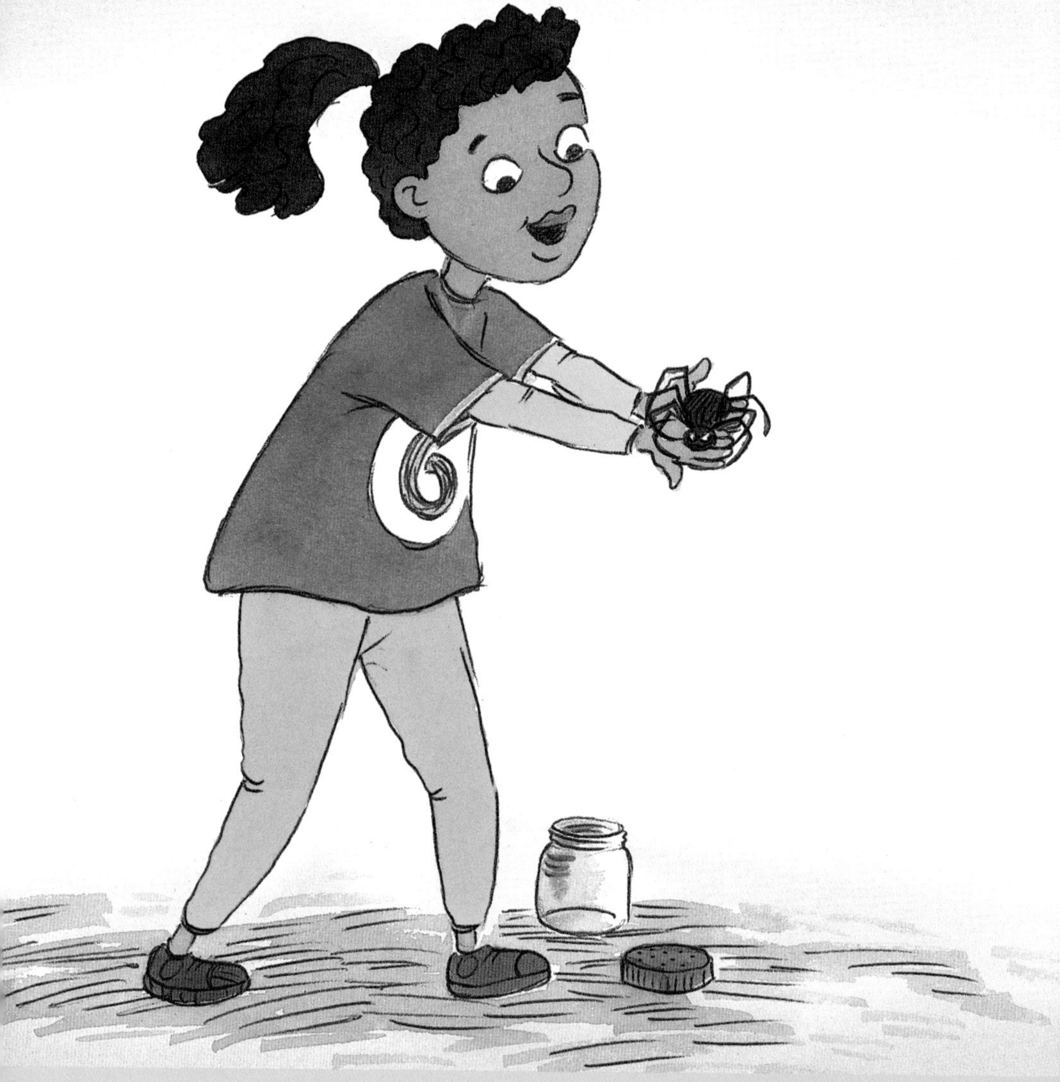

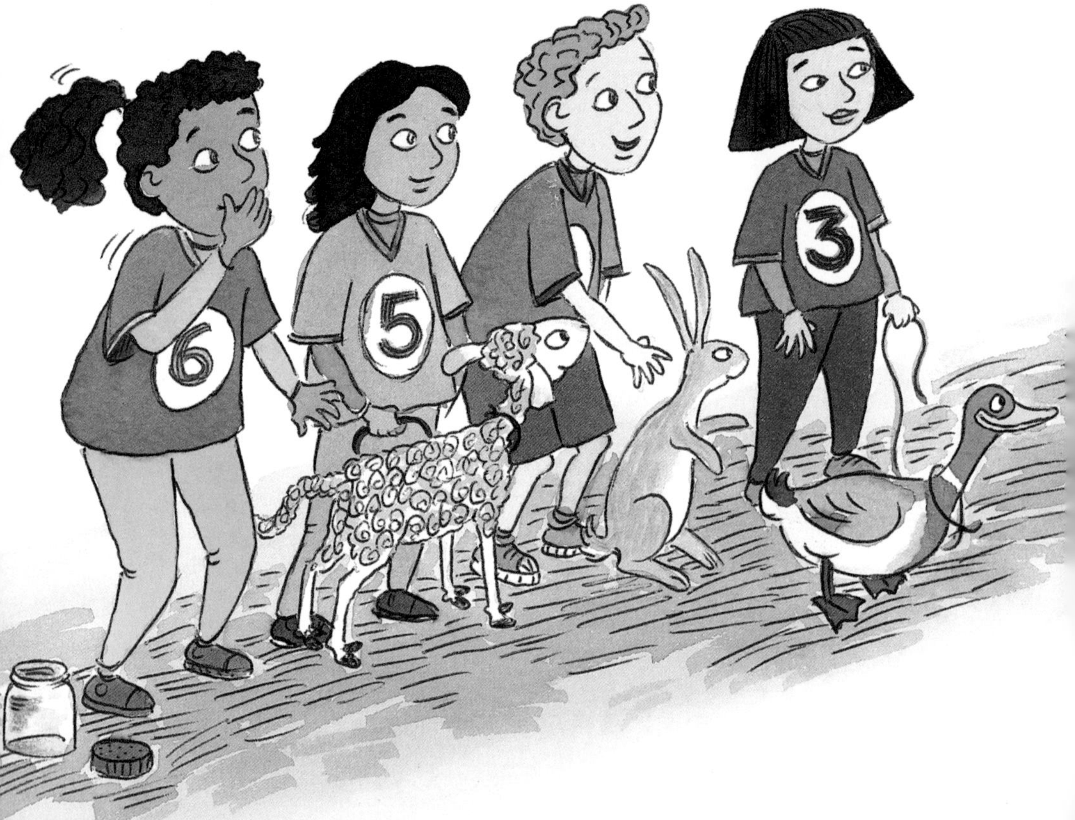
6
5
3

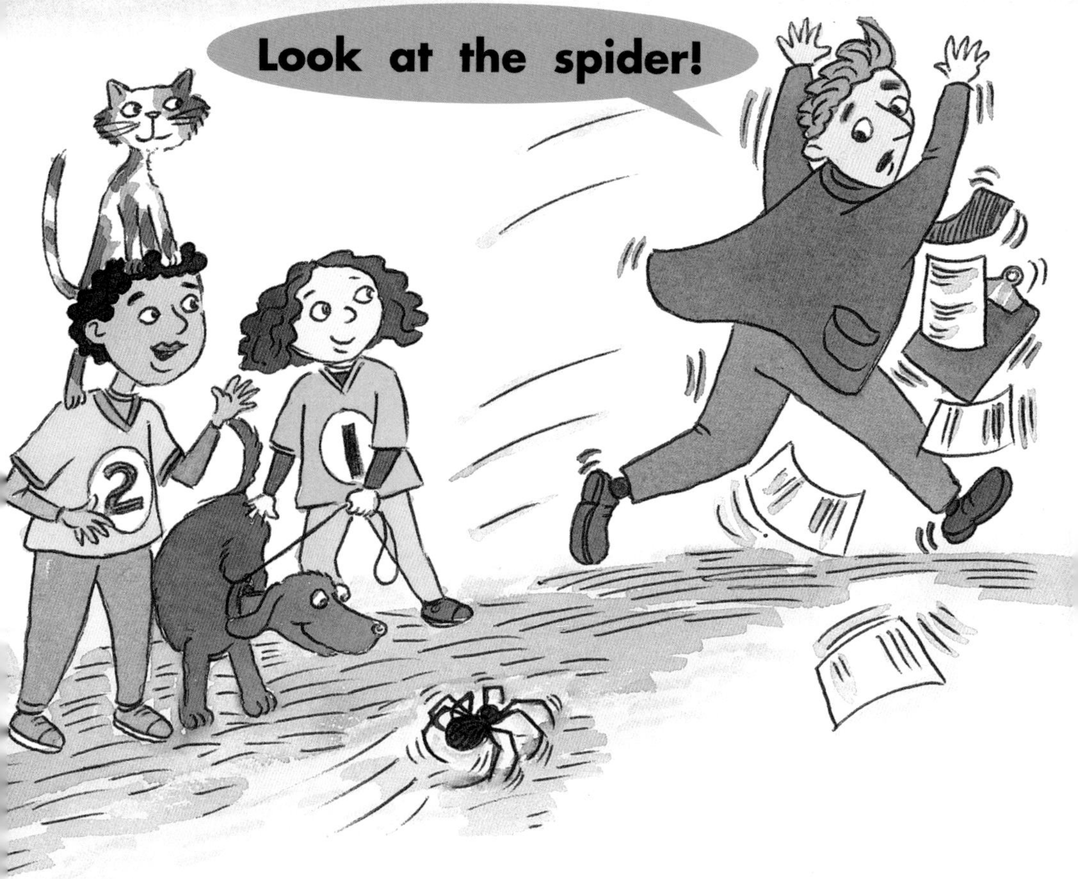
Look at the spider!
2
1

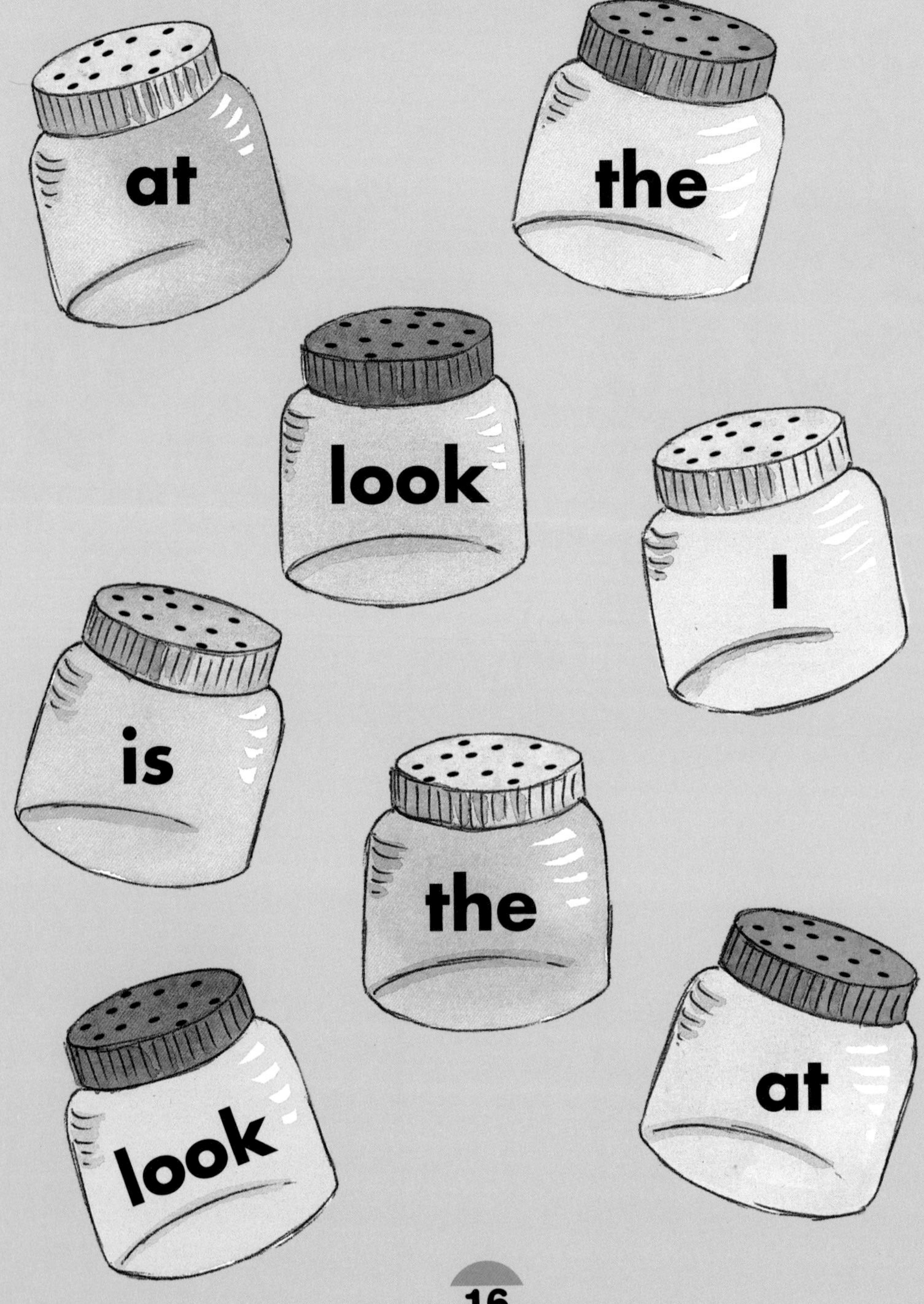
at
the
look
I
is
the
look
at